1594

D0182978

BARN PARTY

CLAIRE O'BRIEN

Illustrated by
TIM ARCHBOLD

Barn party

Kingfisher

KINGFISHER

An imprint of Kingfisher Publications Plc
New Penderel House, 283-288 High Holborn
London WC1V 7HZ

First published by Kingfisher 1996
4 6 8 10 9 7 5
Text copyright © Claire O'Brien 1996
Illustrations copyright © Tim Archbold 1996

Educational Adviser: Prue Goodwin
Reading and Language Centre
University of Reading

A CIP catalogue record for this book
is available from the British Library.

ISBN 0 7534 0020 0

Printed in Singapore

Contents

Chapter One

Cockerel Does A Mean Thing

"Make sure you put that poster up
where everyone will see it,"
called the Chicken Sisters.

Cockerel hung it on the apple tree.

PARTY!
TONIGHT
IN THE BARN
ALL WELCOME!

FROM
THE CHICKEN SISTERS

Then he read it.

PARTY!
TONIGHT
IN THE BARN
ALL WELCOME!

FROM
THE CHICKEN SISTERS

"Oh, no!" thought Cockerel.

"*All* welcome.

That means all the dirty, untidy animals will be there."

"I like things tidy and clean.

They'll spoil it."

Then he did a mean thing.

He crossed out

~~ALL WELCOME!~~

and wrote

By invitation only

The animals gathered round

to read the poster.

7

"By invitation only?"

Pig was puzzled.

"I'm sure we'll all be invited,"
said Duck.

"Yes, we're all
friends here,"
said Goat.

"No one would have a party
without inviting *all* the animals,"
said Cow.

"I'd better have a nap
before the dancing starts,"
said Dog.

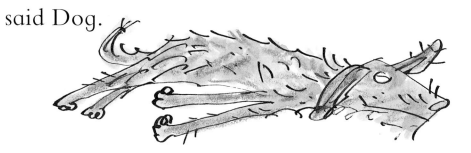

Pig tried on her new ribbon.

"How do I look?" she called to Cockerel.

"It's for the party."

She twirled around her pigpen

to show him her lovely ribbon.

10

"Oh, I'm sorry, but you're not invited,"

said Cockerel.

Pig sank down in the mud.

SPLOP!

"You're just too muddy, I'm afraid.

It's a party for clean, tidy animals."

And he strutted off.

Duck tried on her new bonnet.

"Do I look nice?" she called to Cockerel.

"It's for the party."

She gave a little paddle around her pond

so that he could see her bonnet

from all sides.

12

"Oh, I'm sorry, but you're not invited,"
said Cockerel.

Duck sank down in the water.

SPLUG!

And he strutted off again.

He thought he was doing a fine job.

"It will be a very tidy party,"

he thought. "Tidy and clean."

15

Chapter Two

Cockerel Does More Mean Things

Goat was trying on his new scarf.

He had nibbled a bit of it away.

"I suppose that's for the party,"

said Cockerel, leaning on the fence.

"Yes," giggled Goat. "Do you like it?"
He wrapped it round and round his neck
to show how long it was.

"Very nice," said Cockerel.

"But I'm afraid you're not invited."

Poor Goat.

His head drooped down.

SLUMP!

"You're just too scruffy," said Cockerel.

"And you would nibble everyone's clothes.

It's a party for clean, tidy animals."

And Cockerel strutted off.

Cow had a new set of teeth.

"I just got these in time for the party,"

she called to Cockerel

with a big, toothy smile.

Cockerel thought Cow

was the untidiest animal of all.

He didn't like her dribbly mouth

and her long swishy tail.

He didn't like her big clumsy feet.

He thought she needed a haircut.

"Oh, I'm sorry, you haven't been invited,"

he said, not feeling sorry at all.

"You're just too big and sloppery.

It's a party for clean, tidy animals."

Cow was too upset to say anything.

She SLAMMED the shed door

and went away to cry.

Dog was dozing by the farmhouse door.

He opened one lazy eye

as Cockerel walked past.

Cockerel was afraid of Dog.

"Going to the party?" Dog asked.

"Yes, I am," said Cockerel,

peeking out from behind a plant pot.

"But I'm afraid you're not invited.

You would just fall asleep

or scratch your fleas all the time.

It's a party for clean, tidy animals."

Dog showed his white teeth

and SNARLED at Cockerel.

Cockerel ran away fast.

"Are you going to the party?"
the animals asked each other.

"Cockerel says I'm too muddy,"
said Pig, brushing her ribbon.

"He says I'm too wet and drippy,"

said Duck,

wringing out her bonnet.

"He says I'm too scruffy

and I'd nibble everyone's clothes,"

said Goat, munching a sock

that had blown off the washing line.

"He says I'm too big and sloppery,"
said Cow, washing her new teeth
in a bucket.

"We can have our own party," said Dog,

in the middle of a really good scratch,

"without that mean old Cockerel

and those snooty chicken sisters."

"Brilliant idea!" agreed the others.
So they put their heads together
and planned their own party.

Chapter Three

Cockerel Gets More Than He Expected

The Chicken Sisters were busy

getting the barn ready.

They hung decorations

and swept the floor.

They put out hay bales to sit on

and blew up balloons.

"Why hasn't anyone asked us

about the party?"

wondered Sister Matilda.

"Perhaps they're just too busy

getting all dressed up,"

said Sister Harriet, smiling happily.

Then they saw the poster!

They went to talk to the other animals

straight away.

When they found out

what Cockerel had done

they were furious!

"It's time to teach that Cockerel a lesson!"

said the Chicken Sisters.

All the animals agreed to help.

Cockerel spent all afternoon getting ready.

He had a bubble-bath.

He combed his feathers.

He polished his beak.

He clipped his claws
and he brushed
his best bow-tie.

"You are splendid," he said to himself.

"Tidy and clean and magnificent."

But the other animals

were waiting for him in the barn.

Pig gave him a bucket of mud. SPLAT!

Duck hosed him down. SQUIRT!

Goat chewed his bow-tie. RIP!

Cow kicked up some straw. IT STUCK!

Dog dug up the dust.

COUGH! SPLUTTER!

And the Chicken Sisters

gave him some old eggs. POOHEY!

"Well, now you have no friends at all,"
said the Chickens as they left.

Cockerel was all alone
and he looked terrible.

He was the dirtiest, untidiest animal of all.

And he was MISERABLE!

In Cow's shed, the other animals
got on with their party.

They were having a brilliant time.

After a while, Cockerel came in.

A big tear rolled off his beak.

"I've been a foolish, unfriendly cockerel,"

he said, "and I'm very sorry."

"You can join our party if you like,"
said Pig, gently.

"Yes, please," said Cockerel.
"If I'm not too dirty and messy."
"You're fine just as you are,"
said the others.

So they danced all night.

Pig was muddy.

Duck was wet.

Goat was scruffy and ate Duck's bonnet.

Cow was clumsy

and her tail swished everywhere.

Dog stopped to scratch his fleas

now and then,

but no one minded.

They all enjoyed themselves.

Each animal was different

and they were all good friends.

And Cockerel made sure
that everyone was up early
the next morning
to tidy things up.

About the Author and Illustrator

Claire O'Brien trained as a teacher and has done many jobs in her time including teaching English in Colombia and Drama in the USA. Claire says, "I have met lots of people from all over the world. Some are tidy and some are very messy, just like in this farmyard. They are all different but they are all my friends."

Tim Archbold has illustrated many books for children including a collection of Knock-Knock jokes for Kingfisher. He lives deep in the countryside and says, "I know just how hard it can be to keep clean and tidy, especially when it's muddy. When I take my dog Sam for a walk, there's nothing he likes better than splashing through puddles."

If you've enjoyed reading *Barn Party*,
try these other **I Am Reading** books:

ALLIGATOR TAILS AND CROCODILE CAKES
Nicola Moon & Andy Ellis

GRANDAD'S DINOSAUR
Brough Girling & Stephen Dell

KIT'S CASTLE
Chris Powling & Anthony Lewis

MISS WIRE AND THE THREE KIND MICE
Ian Whybrow & Emma Chichester Clark

MR COOL
Jacqueline Wilson & Stephen Lewis

PRINCESS ROSA'S WINTER
Judy Hindley & Margaret Chamberlain

WATCH OUT, WILLIAM
Kady MacDonald Denton